By MADELYN ROSENBERG

How to Behave
at a
TEA PARTY

Illustrated by HEATHER ROSS

KT KATHERINE TEGEN BOOKS
An Imprint of HarperCollins Publishers

~ **For**

Graham and Karina,
who pour the tea.
And for Butch,
who prefers coffee.
—M.R.

~ **For**

the little girls of 90
William, who really know
how to throw a tea party.
And for Gizmo.
—H.R.

How to Behave at a Tea Party. Text copyright © 2014 by Madelyn
Rosenberg. Illustrations copyright © 2014 by Heather Ross. All rights
reserved. Manufactured in China. No part of this book may be used
or reproduced in any manner whatsoever without written permission
except in the case of brief quotations embodied in critical articles and
reviews. For information address HarperCollins Children's Books, a
division of HarperCollins Publishers, 195 Broadway, New York, NY
10007.
www.harpercollinschildrens.com

Library of Congress Cataloging-in-Publication Data
Rosenberg, Madelyn, 1966–
     How to behave at a tea party / by Madelyn Rosenberg ; illustrated
by Heather Ross. — First edition.
          pages   cm
     Summary: Although Julia instructs her younger brother, Charlie,
and other guests in proper behavior, her tea party does not turn out
as she had planned.
     ISBN 978-0-06-227926-2 (hardcover)
     [1. Etiquette—Fiction.   2. Tea—Fiction.   3. Parties—Fiction.
4. Brothers and sisters—Fiction.   5. Behavior—Fiction.]   I. Ross,
Heather, illustrator.   II. Title.
PZ7.R71897How 2014   2013037272
[E]—dc23

The artist used Photoshop to create the digital illustrations
for this book.
Typography by Martha Rago
14 15 16 17 18   SCP   10 9 8 7 6 5 4 3 2 1
❖
First Edition

First, you open the invitation.

Then, you scrub your left elbow and your right knee.

Don't forget the ears, Charles.

Or the nose.

Next, you put on
fancy clothes.

Wear a fancy hat.

Underwear does not count as a hat.

Help me put out the
tablecloth and a fresh
vase of peonies.

Do NOT invite the
McKagan brothers.

Or the frog.

Leave the snake in your room, Charles.

You may bring a *stuffed* animal. And a present.

Do not eat the peonies.

Or the tablecloth!

You must take deep breaths
and count to seven.

I will do all of the pouring.

You will hold the teacup nicely

by the handle, like this.

We will eat tiny sponge
cakes with raspberry jam and
sandwiches that are cut out
with cookie cutters.

Except for Rexie. You may
bring your own bone.

You must say "please"
and "thank you."

You must NOT slurp like a moose.

Or burp like Uncle Victor.

You must take deeper breaths and count to 382.

You can't build a rocket out of sugar cubes.

Do NOT tie Bearie to the chair.

No towers out of teacups, Charles.

But frogs don't even LIKE tea.

Towers shouldn't—

If you want to have a proper tea party,

you must reinvite the guests.

All right. Go ahead. Bring the
McKagan brothers.

Of course you're invited,
Rexie.

You, too, Frog.

I suppose we *could* build a rocket ship
out of sugar cubes.

Maybe we could make a castle.

And a dragon.

And a moat!

You may juggle the saucers
if you want to, Charles,

and rest a spoon on
your nose.

You may turn your napkin
into a dinosaur and the
tablecloth into a cape.

If it's high tea,
you must drink it
at the tippy top.

And you must give me
a hug and say . . .

Oh, Julia, you *do* throw
the best parties!